MW01130614

EDGE BOOKS

BMX EXTREME

BMX EVENTS

by Brian D. Fiske

Consultant:
Keith Mulligan
Editor/Photographer
TransWorld BMX Magazine

Capstone Press
Mankato, Minnesota

Edge Books are published by Capstone Press
151 Good Counsel Drive, P.O. Box 669, Mankato, Minnesota 56002
www.capstonepress.com

Printed in the United States of America

Library of Congress Cataloging-in-Publication Data
Fiske, Brian D.
BMX events / by Brian D. Fiske.
p. cm.—(Edge books. BMX extreme)
Includes bibliographical references and index.
Contents: BMX competitions—BMX Races—Freestyle events—Riders and classes.
ISBN 0-7368-2433-2 (hardcover)
1. Bicycle motocross—Juvenile literature. [1. Bicycle motocross. 2. Bicycle racing.]
I. Title. II. Series.
GV1049.3.F577 2004
796.6'2—dc22 2003013710

Editorial Credits
Angela Kaelberer, editor; Enoch Peterson, series designer; Jason Knudson, book designer; Jo Miller, photo researcher

Photo Credits
AP Wide World Photos, 5; Andrew Laker, 22
Getty Images/Elsa, 6, 20
James Cassimus, 17
Keith Mulligan/TransWorld BMX, cover, 12, 13, 14, 19, 21, 25, 26
Scot "OM" Breithaupt, 9, 10
SportsChrome-USA/Michael Zito, 29

1 2 3 4 5 6 09 08 07 06 05 04

Table of Contents

CHAPTER 1

BMX Competitions

On August 11, 2002, eight BMX racers balanced on the starting gate at Camp Woodward in Woodward, Pennsylvania. The riders were ready to compete in the main event of downhill BMX at the X Games.

As the gate fell, the riders dropped down 5 feet (1.5 meters) below the gate. They sailed over the track's first jump. After a straightaway full of jumps, the racers carved through a steep 180-degree berm.

Robbie Miranda pulled into the lead, but the other racers were right behind him. As he came onto the last straightaway, Miranda pulled farther ahead.

Learn about:

- Downhill BMX
- Racing and freestyle
- BMX today

Robbie Miranda led the downhill BMX race at the 2002 X Games.

When he took the last jump, Miranda tried to do a trick to entertain the fans. He lost his balance and crashed after he crossed the finish line.

Miranda's fall left him dirty and sore, but he was happy. He had won a gold medal.

Dave Mirra and other freestyle riders compete at the X Games.

BMX History

Riders have been racing BMX bikes since the early 1970s. At first, racers organized their own races at motocross tracks. They often raced for trophies instead of prize money.

By the early 1980s, BMX racing was popular in the United States and Canada. The National Bicycle League (NBL), the American Bicycle Association (ABA), and other groups held BMX races in North America.

Races were not the only BMX competitions. Some riders did tricks and jumps on their bikes. People called this new sport "freestyle." By the 1990s, freestyle had become more popular than BMX racing.

Today, BMX riders still race in NBL and ABA events. They also compete in freestyle contests at the X Games and the Gravity Games. In 2001, the X Games added a BMX downhill race. The NBL and other BMX organizations also put on downhill events. In 2008, BMX races will be part of the Olympic Games.

CHAPTER 2

BMX Races

Motocross racing was popular in the late 1960s. Riders raced motorcycles on dirt tracks, hitting jumps and winding through tight turns.

Many young people liked these motorcycle races. They wanted to do the jumps and turns that the motorcycle riders could do, but they were too young to race motorcycles. Some of these young riders raced their bicycles on motorcycle tracks. They called the sport bicycle motocross, or BMX.

Learn about:

- Early races
- Organizations
- Race systems

BMX began when kids started racing bikes on motocross tracks.

First Races

The first organized BMX race took place in Santa Monica, California, in 1969. A group of kids asked a worker at Palms Park to help them organize a bicycle race. The riders had so much

The 1974 Yamaha Gold Cup Series was the first major BMX event.

fun that they kept coming back to the park to race. Soon, riders in other towns held races.

By the early 1970s, BMX racing needed more organization. The sport needed rules, so racers would know what to expect at each event. Someone also had to keep track of the top racers in the country. These racers could then compete against each other.

National Bicycle Association

In 1973, BMX track owner Ernie Alexander formed the first national BMX organization, the National Bicycle Association (NBA). In 1974, the NBA helped organize the first large BMX event. The races were called the Yamaha Gold Cup Series.

Gold Cup races were held in Los Angeles and San Diego, California. The finals took place in the Los Angeles Coliseum. The dirt track was laid out around a football field. The event was so popular that *Sports Illustrated* magazine did a story about it. The story helped get people all over North America excited about BMX racing.

NBL and ABA

In 1974, George Esser formed the National Bicycle League (NBL). Earlier, Esser had started the National Motorcycle League (NML). His sons were both BMX racers. They asked Esser to start a group like the NML for BMX racers.

Today, the NBL has about 40,000 members. It holds about 25 national races each year. These races lead up to the Grand Nationals in August. Racers call this race the "Grands." In each class, the rider with the most points earns the National Number One title.

Racers call the NBL Grand Nationals the "Grands."

The ABA puts on hundreds of races each year.

With about 60,000 members, the American Bicycle Association (ABA) is the largest BMX organization in the United States. The ABA formed in 1977 and puts on hundreds of races every year. It also has its own series of national races and events.

In the transfer system, riders have three chances to qualify.

BMX Race Systems

The biggest difference between the NBL and the ABA is the system they use to run their races. The NBL uses the moto system. The ABA uses the transfer system.

With both systems, the basic race is the same. Racers line up on the starting gate and ride as fast as they can to the finish line. When more than one group of racers compete, the event includes a series of races. In the main event, the best racers compete against each other.

In the moto system, each racer in a group must race in three races called motos. The first-place racer earns one point. Each other racer receives two or more points according to their finish. The racers with the fewest points move up to the semifinals or semis. The semis winners then compete in the main event. Depending on the number of racers, riders may need to compete in earlier races called qualifying rounds.

In the transfer system, a rider has three chances to qualify for the main event. Racers must finish first or second in one of their races in order to move on to the semis or main event.

CHAPTER 3

Freestyle Events

Jumps and tricks have been part of BMX since the beginning of the sport. But it was not until 1979 that freestyle riding had its first official riders. That year, *BMX ACTION* magazine asked Bob Haro and R. L. Osborn to form the *BMX ACTION* Trick Team. Haro and Osborn put on shows for fans all over the United States. They also appeared on TV.

Learn about:

- ***BMX ACTION* Trick Team**
- **Early events**
- **Freestyle today**

R. L. Osborn was one of the first freestyle BMX riders.

Freestyle Growth

Freestyle became more popular in the 1980s. Riders took their bikes to skateboard parks to practice tricks on ramps and halfpipes. Soon, they started holding their own contests to see who could jump the highest and do the best tricks. Before long, these small events turned into real competitions. Judges gave riders scores on their tricks.

By the mid-1980s, several BMX companies put on freestyle events. But freestyle's popularity did not explode until the X Games came along.

Major Events

Freestyle BMX events have been a part of the X Games since the first competition in 1995. In 2000, the NBC TV network started a similar competition called the Gravity Games.

Freestyle riders do handplants and other tricks at the X Games.

Vert riders use halfpipe ramps to do tricks.

Today, freestyle riders compete in four types of events. Vert riders do tricks on large halfpipe ramps. Park riders compete on courses with obstacles such as ramps and box jumps. Flatland riders do balancing tricks on parking lots and other flat, paved surfaces. Dirt riders do tricks in the air over mounds of dirt called doubles.

FACT:

Many bike companies sponsor trick teams. These teams often perform at bike shops, state fairs, and halftime shows at sports events.

Dirt riders do tricks on jumps made of dirt.

In 2002, Mat Hoffman showed his skill at the Boom Boom HuckJam.

Boom Boom HuckJam

Not all BMX events are competitions. Some events are simply a way for riders to put on a show for the fans. One of these events is Tony Hawk's Boom Boom HuckJam.

In 2002, skateboarder Tony Hawk decided to put on a show that combined music and freestyle tricks. Hawk asked some of his skateboard, BMX, and motocross friends to join him in the show. The Boom Boom HuckJam has appeared in many large cities in the United States and Canada.

CHAPTER 4

Riders and Classes

Many major BMX events are for pro riders. These riders are skilled enough to earn a living from the sport.

Most pro riders are sponsored. Sponsoring companies give money and products to riders. In return, riders use the companies' products. Riders also have the companies' names or logos on their clothing or bikes. Amateur riders also can be sponsored. They usually do not earn a living from competitions and sponsorships.

Some large BMX events have competitions for both pro and amateur racers. Amateur riders also compete in smaller events organized just for them.

Learn about:

- Sponsorship
- Skill levels
- Organizing events

Riders have sponsors' logos on their clothing and bikes.

Classes

Amateur racers are divided into three groups based on skill level. Beginning racers compete at the novice level. After they gain skill and experience, they move up to the intermediate level. Expert is the highest amateur level. In each

Top riders race in the pro class.

class, riders race against others of the same age. Male and female riders race in separate classes.

The top riders race at the pro level, with separate classes for men and women. Pro classes are also broken down by experience level.

Many freestyle events are also divided into classes. Pro and amateur riders often compete in different classes. Some freestyle events also separate riders by age.

Local Events

The ABA and the NBL put on most BMX races, even small local events. These groups make sure that the races are fair and safe.

Riders have more freedom to organize local freestyle events. At small events, riders set up obstacles and ramps in an empty parking lot or large driveway. Larger competitions can be held in bike or skateboard parks.

Riders can ask a local bike shop to help pay for and advertise the event. With food, music, and prizes, local events can be as fun for riders and fans as large events shown on TV.

Event Safety

People who organize events need to make sure the events are safe. Riders should wear helmets. They also should wear pads on their knees, elbows, and shins. Ramps need to be sturdy enough to support riders and the impact of their jumps and tricks. The organizers could be responsible if a rider or fan is hurt because of a problem with the course or equipment.

BMX events are fun for riders and fans. As long as riders push the limits of what can be done on a bike, the sport will continue to grow.

Riders wear pads on their elbows, knees, and shins.

Glossary

amateur (AM-uh-chur)—an athlete who usually does not earn a living from participating in a sport

berm (BURM)—a banked turn or corner on a BMX track

intermediate (in-tur-MEE-dee-it)—a competitive class for amateur riders who have the skills to move out of the novice class

motocross (MOH-toh-kross)—a sport in which people race motorcycles on dirt tracks

novice (NOV-iss)—a competitive class for beginning amateur riders

obstacle (OB-stuh-kuhl)—an object such as a ramp or railing; park BMX riders do tricks on obstacles.

straightaway (STRAYT-uh-way)—a straight area of a BMX track

Read More

Blomquist, Christopher. *BMX in the X Games.* A Kid's Guide to the X Games. New York: PowerKids Press, 2003.

Herran, Joe, and Ron Thomas. *BMX Riding.* Action Sports. Philadelphia: Chelsea House, 2003.

Nelson, Julie. *BMX Racing and Freestyle.* Extreme Sports. Austin, Texas: Steadwell Books, 2002.

Useful Addresses

American Bicycle Association
P.O. Box 718
Chandler, AZ 85244

National Bicycle League
3958 Brown Park Drive, Suite D
Hilliard, OH 43026

TransWorld BMX
1421 Edinger Avenue, Suite D
Tustin, CA 92780

Internet Sites

FactHound offers a safe, fun way to find Internet sites related to this book. All of the sites on FactHound have been researched by our staff.

Here's how:

1. Visit *www.facthound.com*
2. Type in this special code **0736824332** for age-appropriate sites. Or enter a search word related to this book for a more general search.
3. Click on the **Fetch It** button.

FactHound will fetch the best sites for you!

WWW.FACTHOUND.COM SM

Index